IMAGINE THAT™

Licensed exclusively to Imagine That Publishing Ltd
Tide Mill Way, Woodbridge, Suffolk, IP12 1AP, UK
www.imaginethat.com
Copyright © 2021 Imagine That Group Ltd
All rights reserved
0 2 4 6 8 9 7 5 3 1
Manufactured in China

Written by Susie Linn
Illustrated by Adam Horsepool

ISBN 978-1-80105-175-0

A catalogue record for this book is available from the British Library

DINO CLAUS

A TALE OF CHRISTMAS MAGIC

Written by
SUSIE LINN

Illustrated by
ADAM HORSEPOOL

It was December and everyone was excited about Christmas – everyone except Tiny, the little T. rex.

Tiny didn't believe in Christmas magic one little bit!

Daddy Rex loved Christmas more than anything!
He couldn't wait to read his own favourite Christmas
stories to Tiny at bedtime, but Tiny wasn't interested!

'Once Upon a Sleigh Ride,'
suggested Daddy Rex.

'No thanks,'
said Tiny.

'What about, *The Snowman that Came to Life?*' tried Daddy Rex.

'**No!**' grumbled Tiny.

'You might like, *The Elves that Saved Christmas*,' said Daddy Rex, hopefully.

Tiny said nothing.

He looked **VERY** cross!

'Maybe, *The Night Before Christmas?*'
whispered Daddy Rex.

'No, **NO, NO!**'
roared Tiny,
grumpily.

On Christmas Eve, more snow began
to fall outside Tiny's cosy cave.
Suddenly, Tiny heard a jingling
and a jangling in the dark.
He heard the clatter of
hooves on rock!

Whoever, or whatever,
could that be?

Tiny peeped bravely out
at the entrance to his cave.

First, a brown furry
face appeared, then
some wiggly antlers!
Was that ...
a reindeer?

Then a big sack,
bulging with presents,
landed on the cave floor!

Finally, a deep, jolly voice cried,
'Ho, HO, HO!'

A red hat with a white pom-pom appeared,
followed by the toothy, grinning face of big,
friendly ... Dino Claus!

'Happy Christmas, Tiny!'
bellowed Dino Claus,
cheerfully. Tiny
just stared.

'I normally make sure no one sees me,'
continued Dino Claus, 'but I heard that you don't
believe in Christmas magic. It's time we had a chat.'

'Go on! Ask me anything you like,' said Dino Claus. So Tiny took a deep breath and began ...

Dino Claus
answered all of
Tiny's questions,
until finally
it was time for
him to go.

'I still have lots of presents to deliver,' said Dino Claus, kindly. 'Now go to sleep. I'll come back to see you again next year.'

And with that he placed the sack of presents by Tiny's bed, tucked him in and headed out into the snowy night.

Early on
Christmas
morning,
Daddy Rex
was woken by
Tiny jumping
on him, excitedly.

'Daddy! Look!'
cried Tiny. 'It's a book
from Dino Claus!'

It's called,
The Most Magical
Christmas. Can we read it, please?'

Daddy Rex grinned, wiped the sleep
out of his eyes and began ...

'Once upon a time, there was a little dinosaur who didn't believe in Christmas ...'

Tiny cuddled up happily and sighed.

'I love Christmas,' he whispered.